Myrtle of Willendorf

Myrtle of
Willendorf
Rebecca O'Connell

Front Street
Asheville, North Carolina
2000

Library of Congress Cataloging-in-Publication Data

O'Connell, Rebecca
Myrtle of Willendorf / Rebecca O'Connell.—1st ed.
p.cm.
Summary: A bright and artisitc young woman with a
fondness for junk food experiences a kooky modern-day
coming of age by way of the Goddess within.
ISBN 1-886910-52-9 (alk. paper)
[1.Goddess religion—Fiction. 2. Self-acceptance—Fiction.
3. Body image—Fiction. 4. Overweight persons—Fiction.
5. Friendship—Fiction. 6. Coming of age—Fiction.] I. Title
PZ7.02167 My 2000
[fic]—dc21
00-029386

for John

Myrtle of Willendorf

Prologue: The Coven

"Won't you join our coven?" Margie Martin asked me one sunny September afternoon in our junior year.

"Well, Margie, you know me. I've never really been much of a joiner," I replied.

"Just come to our ceremony on Saturday."

Margie and I had become friendly after discovering that we both read mythology the way our classmates pored over *Mademoiselle* and *Seventeen*. But Margie was a practicing pagan, whereas I was merely interested in the classical roots of the Western tradition. And now Margie wanted me to come to a ceremony.

It wasn't like I had a date with the captain of the football team or an important awards banquet to attend, so at 7:30 the following Saturday I rang Margie's doorbell. Mrs. Martin told me, "Go on down to The Den, dear."

Margie's house had a furnished basement which they called The Den. That night, though, I thought it looked more like The Sepulcher. The only light came from four candles the size of coffee cans spaced evenly atop the family's upright piano. The piano was draped with an ornate Indian-print bedspread that transformed it into some sort of altar.

Besides the bayberry candles, the piano supported an assortment of what I supposed were the tools of the trade— I mean, craft. There was a blue glass bottle filled with some clear liquid, a peacock feather, a potted geranium, an unlit white votive candle, and a little lacquered box.

Margie was seated in front of the altar. She usually kept her hair in a long braid, but tonight she had it brushed out like a shiny cape. The look was a little disconcerting, because Margie's hair and eyes were the same color. Lots of people have brown hair and brown eyes, but usually they're two different shades of brown. Margie's eyes were gold, and her hair was the exact same hue, not blond but a very, very light brown. I knew it wasn't fake; Mrs. Martin had the exact same coloring.

Margie sat facing a semicircle of three chairs. Two were occupied by girls I barely knew. I guessed the third was for me.

"Welcome, Myrtle," said Margie very formally, with a sweeping gesture toward the empty chair. I sat down and raised my eyebrows in greeting to the girl on my right, Bobbie Sedge.

Bobbie and I had been friends back in fourth grade when we agitated for animal rights on behalf of the classroom fish and hamsters. The fifth-grade classroom had no pets, and Bobbie and I drifted apart. Now, in eleventh grade, we inhabited completely different social strata. I was a solitary artist, and Bobbie was in the eco-political set. She sported a bracelet made of genuine hemp and campaigned for more vegetarian choices in the cafeteria. I was surprised to see her here. I didn't know Margie even knew her.

If I was surprised to see Bobbie, I was shocked to recognize the girl on my left. Sheila Kurtz had been the only student in the history of Seneca High School to bring her infant daughter to the junior prom. Sheila was a year ahead of me (in school; she was about ten years ahead of me in life experience), and we never had any classes together. I couldn't recall ever speaking with her or, for that matter, seeing her at a distance of less than twelve feet. But she leaned over, gave my arm a warm squeeze, and said, "Hi, Myr. Glad you could make it."

Margie held her hands out, palms up. Bobbie and Sheila each took one and looked at me. I gave my right and left hands to Bobbie and Sheila, respectively. Bobbie's hand was dry and cold and armored with silver rings. Sheila's felt like a warm baked potato.

Margie closed her eyes and intoned, "We have gathered this evening to honor the Goddess as she is manifest in our world and in ourselves.

"The Goddess is the personification of the life force in all things. The Goddess-power is in each of us."

As Margie spoke, Bobbie squared her shoulders; Sheila lifted her chin. Margie continued in that same serious voice, "The life force is female. Ancient people knew this and worshipped a female deity. They saw that new life came from women's bodies and was nurtured at women's breasts. This was beautiful to them. Women's bodies meant life. Life was to be celebrated, and women's bodies were to be celebrated.

"Women's bellies, women's breasts, women's hips, thighs, buttocks. This was the cradle of life; they should be full, rich, lush."

Margie was panting a little now, and her cheeks were flushed. Bobbie leaned back in her chair, eyes closed, a Mona Lisa smile on her lips. Sheila stared at Margie and nodded rapidly, squeezing my hand at each downbeat.

Margie caught her breath and continued, "We see the beauty of the Goddess in every aspect of the natural world. Hence, we welcome the spirit of the Goddess into our circle with the four elements of Nature.

"Fire."

Margie produced a match from somewhere and lit the white candle from the altar. It was coconut scented. She handed it to Bobbie. Bobbie handed it to me. I gave it to Sheila, who passed it to Margie, who replaced it on the altar and picked up the feather.

"Air."

The feather made its way around the circle, and so it went with the blue bottle ("Water") and the geranium ("Earth").

The last item on the altar was the lacquered box. Margie set it on her lap and opened the lid. Inside was a carved figure. It looked like a miniature obese woman. It had itty-bitty arms folded over enormous round breasts. Beneath that was a wide, round abdomen, so the torso looked like two big grapes stuck onto a small plum. Her short, tapered legs seemed to end at the knees, and atop all that was a little bumpy knob for a head.

"Ha! That looks like me right before I had Jilly," said Sheila.

That looks like me right now, I thought.

"This is how ancient people imagined the Goddess," said Margie. "Before God was a pale, thin man, people worshipped a robust, bountiful woman. This is the Venus of Willendorf. Archaeologists found the original in Willendorf, Austria. She is over twenty-five thousand years old. Dozens of similar sculptures have been found all over Europe. She was the Goddess of Neolithic people, the original deity worshipped by humans."

Margie picked up the figure and cradled it in two hands. She looked at it, but she was speaking to us.

"Since then," she said, "patriarchal religion has tried to obliterate Goddess worship but never fully succeeded. Throughout the ages, all over the world, women like us have gathered to honor the Goddess and honor her power, our power."

This concluded the spiritual-ecstasy portion of the

meeting, and we shortly turned to a discussion of the upcoming harvest celebration. We adjourned upon Mrs. Martin's arrival with Hawaiian Punch and pineapple upside-down cake.

Margie was herself a fruitcake. But she was nice, and there was something about this ceremony I liked. I'd always been kind of attached to Artemis, the virgin huntress, and Athena, the gray-eyed embodiment of wisdom. The way Margie told it, they were all facets of the one Goddess we honored at our meetings.

I went back to Margie's the next week, and the next. Sheila was too busy with her baby to attend with any regularity, and Bobbie's interest in women's mysteries waned as her interest in the president of the vegetarian club waxed. By Thanksgiving, Margie and I had become the core membership of Seneca High's coven.

I stayed in all of my junior and most of my senior year, close to one hundred Saturday nights spent in The Den. Maybe that's why, even after everything that happened, Margie still wants to be friends. She sends me e-mail sometimes, postcards too.

I never write back.

Below Protozoa

I should have been taking notes on the biology lecture, but I filled my binder with sketches instead. I drew a strapping young paramecium offering a bouquet to a sweet, shy paramecium whose cilia were swept up in a flattering coif.

Paramecia mate. That's not fair. They taught us in high school that paramecia, single-celled creatures that live in pond water, reproduce asexually. When they need to be fruitful and multiply, they simply split in two. We even got to see it happen under the microscope. Now, two years later, in Bio 101, I was learning that paramecia can reproduce sexually, too. This really bothered me.

I was the only living creature on the face of the Earth

who didn't get to pair off and mate. I was below protozoa on the scale of social evolution. I was literally less romantically adept than pond scum.

I couldn't take this kind of stress. I would have to stop and get an ice cream on my way back to the house I shared with Jada.

Freshmen are required to live on campus. If you don't fill out a roommate request form—and I didn't—you are randomly assigned. I got Jada. We did our two semesters in McLeod Hall, and now we were sophomores, subletting a house for the summer.

It's the kind of thing you do to yourself, like slamming your hand in a car door or volunteering to look after your neighbors' pet cockatiel while they're on vacation. I was contractually bound to live with Jada from May 18 through August 20, and I had no one but myself to blame.

Jada's primary motivation for moving off campus had been to get a room where she could be alone with her boyfriend, Keith Capri, a.k.a. Goat (for his devotion to the sport of rock climbing). She only invited me along to share the rent. I tried not to let this bother me, but without much success. Lately I had been seeking solace in double chocolate cones more and more often.

17

Licking my fingers and savoring the lingering flavor of cocoa and butterfat, I trudged up the back steps and into the kitchen.

"Hey, Myr," Jada called from upstairs, "you got some mail. I put it on the kitchen table for you."

Maybe Jada and I weren't really so different. We shared a similar philosophy of coping with the slings and arrows of outrageous fortune. She had a T-shirt that said, "When the going gets tough, the tough go shopping." Change "shopping" to "eating," and it was a motto I could adopt as my own.

We were in complete agreement about the housework, too. The state of the kitchen was a testimonial to our compatibility. The sink held a crusty pasta pot (Jada's), a greasy frying pan (mine), assorted vegetable peelings (Jada's), and a lump of instant mashed potatoes (mine). I could almost see wavy smell-lines wafting up from it. Perhaps I'd just step back onto the porch for a minute. I picked up the postcard and brought it outside.

How appropriate: a postcard from Margie Martin. My day had already included such pleasures as seismic menstrual cramps, a devastating biology lesson, and a leaky sugar cone. Might as well add on a postcard from a kook.

The Lincoln Memorial. That almost made sense. The Washington Monument she would have considered too phallic. Jefferson had owned slaves, and the White House was the home of he who embodied the white male power structure. Still, it surprised me that she had selected our sixteenth president—another dead white male, a pawn and perpetrator of the patriarchy—to bring me her news. I would have expected, maybe, a close-up of the famous cherry blossoms with Margie's added caption, "The vulva of the Goddess."

Margie had written to say that she had a summer job in Washington, D.C., fundraising for an international relief agency. How mainstream of her. I wondered what she wore to work. I wondered if she still had her menstruation dress. Shortly after my first coven meeting, Margie had appeared, breathless, at my front door carrying this wondrous garment.

"It cost eighty dollars, but I don't regret spending one penny of it!" she said. "I will wear it in honor of the Goddess!"

She unfurled a blue corduroy jumper with red and purple peonies appliquéd to the front pocket.

"So I can celebrate my days of power!" she said.

I folded the postcard and put it in my pocket. I didn't know why she kept sending them to me. Couldn't she take a hint?

I looked around our rickety wooden porch. Jada had a jar of sun tea brewing. I wondered where she'd found such a monster. The jar looked like it had originally held about six quarts of mayonnaise, not that Jada would ever have owned a jar of mayonnaise. As long as I had known her, no oil-based food had ever sullied the gullet of Jada Damascene. My roommate subsisted on iced tea, fresh vegetables, and whole wheat pasta. She looked upon my diet of pizza, ice cream, and canned ravioli as some exotic and revolting cuisine. One night I offered her a Pepsi. A normal roommate would have graciously accepted or politely declined, but Jada acted as if I had offered her a glass of termite milk. She even made a tiny, presumably involuntary, gagging sound. The thought of all those empty calories made her physically ill.

I stared at the jar and thought about Jada.

I heard, Clink, clink-clink, SPLASH!, and then the jar wasn't there anymore, and my legs, socks, and tennis shoes were soaked with warm tea.

Sun Tea

"Oh, Myr! Are you okay?" Jada had heard the crash and came out onto the porch.

She looked like she was on her way to rehearsal. Jada was one of the few who could look graceful in a pair of bulky rubber pants. She said that they were to keep her muscles warm. It was supposed to go to 85 degrees today, but she was wearing her rubber pants. She was also wearing a black leotard and a concerned expression.

"I'm sorry about your sun tea," I said. "I don't know what happened."

"Don't worry about the tea, but honestly, you're way too stressed out. You should exercise more. Work off your tension. Physical fitness is not just about being in good shape. It adds grace and confidence, so you don't bump into things!"

I'm sure Jada meant well, but I couldn't concentrate on what she was saying. It was hard to have a conversation with Jada because I always felt like I was engaging in discourse with a llama. She would have blended right into a herd: long, flexible neck, large, lavishly lashed eyes, soft black hair in corkscrew curls. She looked just like one.

"Jada, the thing is, I didn't knock it over. I was standing by the steps when I ..."

I couldn't quite tell her when what. I couldn't quite say, "when I caused the jar to break by tapping into my natural mystical powers and beaming destructive thought waves at it." The idea was too hard to take seriously. Even I, with two years of coven-based instruction behind me, didn't really believe it. But I had a creeping suspicion it was true.

Jada tried to help me out, "It fell? When the jar fell?" she said.

"Well," I said, "the jar didn't exactly fall. I know this sounds crazy, but it, like, disintegrated. When I looked at it."

She appeared to ruminate on this idea for a few moments, then asked, "Do you think your feet on the steps could have, you know ..."

What she meant was, "Do you think it is possible that you're so heavy that your footfalls actually shook the porch and toppled the jar?" But she was having trouble finding a way to put it diplomatically, so she tried another approach.

"You mean you just looked at the jar and broke it?" she said.

"I know what you're thinking, but that's clocks, not jars of tea."

A blank look from Jada, and then she turned tail (I almost expected to see a short, furry tail, but it was just her rubber-clad dancer's rump) and walked over to the pile of broken glass and sodden tea bags at the edge of the porch. She crouched by the evidence in a flat-footed squat.

"And you're sure you didn't accidentally push it?" she asked.

"I'm sure." What did she think I was? Some kind of mad jar-smasher?

"Well, then, there's only one possible explanation."

Jada stood up and came back to where I was standing. I had learned over the better part of a semester to tell when Jada was being facetious. It had to do with the way she held her long, long neck. She was holding it that way now and

23

smiling a goofy llama-smile.

"Golly, Myr! Better alert the authorities. Here we have a proven case of telekinesis! You'll be famous, hounded by the press!"

Without bending her knees, Jada bent down and picked up a hairbrush that someone left on the porch long ago. She held it like a microphone and said in a deep voice, "We are here on the porch where college student and aspiring artist Myrtle Parcittadino has just exploded a jar using only the power of concentration. Tell us, Myr, where did you get the power to move things with your mind?"

I thought about how the jar had just kind of crumpled under my gaze. I thought about the postcard in my back pocket, and I thought seriously about an answer for Jada.

"It's my moon time," I told her.

Moon Time

"Moon time" was Margie's way of saying menstrual period. She always maintained that a woman's monthly cycle was beauteous and miraculous, something to be celebrated and consecrated. She liked to tell Bobbie, Sheila, and me about an order of nuns who embroidered flowers, geometric patterns, and sacred verses on their menstrual pads.

"I'd like to do that too," she would say wistfully, "but I would have to spend all my time just stitching and stitching."

Margie was proud of her copious flow. It wasn't unusual, she told us with mock humility, for her moon times to last six or seven days. Mine seldom lasted less than a week, but I didn't brag. I thought that was between me and the Goddess.

I remembered Margie holding forth on this topic at one of the early coven meetings.

"Your moon time is your time of strength, when your mystical powers are at their height," she told us. Coven meetings were different from ceremonies. We still met in The Den at Margie's, but the piano was undraped. The lights were on, and we had another white votive candle burning to symbolize the glow of the Goddess. I thought this one was vanilla scented, but it was hard to tell because Mrs. Martin had provided the coven with a platter of blondies, and the aroma that filled the room might just as easily have come from them. Sheila, Bobbie, and I consumed these gifts of the Goddess's bounty and attended to Margie's lecture.

"You can learn to recognize the energy of the Goddess concentrated in your muscles at this time of the cycle. During your moon time, be aware of a tightness in your lower back and abdomen. This is stored Goddess-energy."

"Sounds like cramps," I said.

"Myrtle, you live in a patriarchal culture. You have been conditioned to perceive Goddess-energy as pain, all the more so because you respond to the energy with tension instead of joy.

"When you feel the Goddess's strength coiled in your belly, try to welcome the sensation instead of automatically reaching for the Midol. Open yourself to the experience. Let the Goddess-energy flow through you with your menstrual blood. If you celebrate your power instead of stifling it, your moon time will be a time of joy and pleasure for you!"

"Definitely," said Bobbie. "It's true about the Goddess-energy. I read where women are four times more likely to win the lottery if they buy the ticket during their period."

Sheila nodded in solemn agreement. "My aunt once told me that her biggest bingo winnings are always when she's got her period."

"So the Goddess is a gambler?" I asked.

Margie ignored my irreverent tone and seized the opportunity to teach.

"The Goddess is not a gambler, but her energy can influence the physical sphere. Many menstruating women find that their energy affects their surroundings. Lights burn brighter, dishes break, books fall open to special pages, things like that. Many of us are slightly telekinetic all month, and the Goddess amplifies our power at our moon times."

Warm Jungle Rain

Jada wearied of the sun tea investigation and went back inside. I swept the ruins of the jar into a dustpan with the brush Jada had used to interview me.

Jada went out to rehearsal. I stayed in and enjoyed the solitude.

The next morning I awoke from a vivid dream. I dreamt I was in the jungle, standing under the broad leaf of a banana tree. It was raining hard, and the leaf above me magnified the sound of the rain. It didn't keep the rain off me, though, and I felt it on my thighs.

That's when my eyes snapped open and the sound of the rain became the shower running across the hall.

I cursed my alarm clock. It must have allowed me to sleep into Jada's bathroom time. When Jada went into the bathroom she stayed there for two hours. Besides completing the usual elimination and hygiene tasks, she shaved her legs, plucked her brows, and waxed her bikini area. She conditioned her hair, revitalized her skin, and moisturized her lips. She applied color to her cheekbones, lacquer to her toenails, and lenses to her eyeballs.

I knew all this because she had often tried to recruit me into her cosmetic cult. I resisted, but she was devoted and never missed her morning ritual. Weekdays, it lasted from 7:00 a.m. to 9:00 a.m. That meant that if I woke up at 7:01, I had to wait till 9:01 to pee. For this reason I always got up at 6:40, occupied the bathroom for twenty minutes, and then relinquished it to Jada.

I had overslept. Ordinarily this would have been annoying, but now it was alarming. What in my dream was warm jungle rain between my legs, in reality was fresh red blood. My poor maxipad lay in a great big puddle of blood all around. Oh pity the maxi, all covered in gore. It couldn't absorb one milliliter more.

All my supplies were in the bathroom. I would just have to interrupt Jada's bathroom time and hope to escape without a lecture on the benefits of exfoliating regularly. I put on my robe and stepped into the hallway.

Jada sometimes did stretching exercises in the shower; she said the hot water loosened her muscles. I heard her doing them now. Beneath the sound of the shower turned on full blast was a quiet thump-thump.

I tapped on the door and said to it, "Jada, I just have to come in for a minute, okay?"

No answer. I was sure she couldn't hear me over the water, so I opened the door and called into the steam, "Jada, I have to come in and get something, okay?" and entered the bathroom.

I rummaged around in my drawer for what I needed. Jada's boxes and jars of beauty products were encroaching on my storage space, but eventually I unearthed my pads. At that moment the water stopped running and I heard the shower curtain open behind me.

I started to explain, pads held high to show Jada my justification for being there. "Not to invade your privacy, Jada, but I'm bleeding profusely, and I just had to get in here and … Omigod!"

I had turned around to see Jada take two towels off the rack, wrap one around herself, and hand the other one to Goat.

I lunged for the door, smashing my shin on the toilet. As I threw my arms out to catch my balance, my pads went sailing toward the tub.

Rock climbers need quick reflexes. Goat reached out and picked my pads from the air before him.

He held my pads out to me and I took them just as casually as if he had the towel around his waist instead of draped over his neck.

"Nice catch," I told him.

This time I made it through the door without bumping into any bathroom fixtures. The air in the hallway was sweet and dry after the humid and strangely pungent bathroom. I leaned against the wall and waited for my heart to slow down enough that I could make the four steps back to my room without collapsing. Behind me and through the wall I heard Goat and Jada.

"Is she okay?" said Goat.

"Oh, sure. You probably gave her the thrill of a lifetime," said Jada.

"I think she was really embarrassed."

"Well, she shouldn't be. It's no big deal," said Jada. Don't sweat the small stuff. Jada's words to live by.

I heard them walk toward the door, which sent me to my room in a hurry. I still needed the bathroom, but I couldn't face them in the hallway.

Back in my room, I searched for my clock with the idea that I would punish it for subjecting me to that scene. But when I found it, it read only 6:50. My seldom-worn wristwatch confirmed the time. I hadn't invaded Jada's bathroom time; she had invaded mine.

Green  Eggs and Ham

I was not nearly cool enough to be seen in Horton's after 10:00 a.m. Horton's was a coffee shop with a grill and a Dr. Seuss motif. Posters of the Grinch and the Cat in the Hat were a real draw, and by midmorning every day the staff of the university's alternative newspaper had taken possession of the two front tables. From then on, you couldn't get so much as a cup of Yertle the Turtle soup in that place unless you were a student activist, a member of an indie band, or seeing one or more of the above. Once the VIPs were served, there simply wasn't any more seating.

Jada and Goat had no trouble getting a seat at Horton's. Not only did they have sufficiently high coolness quotients, they were in tight with Seth and Julie, the editors of the alternative paper. In theory, Goat and Seth were roommates. They shared a tiny apartment a block or so from our sublet. Julie lived with about six other women in a high-rise on the other side of campus. In practice, Julie and Seth usually stayed at the apartment, and Goat usually stayed with Jada. The four of them often hung around Horton's between classes.

But at least I was free to enjoy Horton's cuisine anytime between 7:00 and 10:00 a.m. Once I again had access to the bathroom, I showered, dressed, and went to Horton's for breakfast.

"Good morning, Myr!" said Sam. I had been devouring plates of Sam's green eggs and ham since the previous September.

Sam was the most dapper fry cook I had ever seen. Today he was spiffy as ever in tan slacks, a neatly tucked chambray shirt, and, as usual, a tie that would make a circus poster look monochromatic. His taste in ties and his outsize mustache made him look more like a children's TV personality than a restaurateur. Sam had taught elementary school for seven years before retiring to open his omelet shop.

"So, when are you going to lend me one of your beautiful pictures to put up in here?" Sam asked when I sat down at the counter.

"It would be arrogant of me to hang my work among such immortals," I said, nodding toward a picture of the Lorax.

"No, I'm planning to take the Seuss stuff down for a while," said Sam. "Horton's is going to host an art show. There's going to be an opening next week, with hors d'oeuvres, champagne, the works! I feed a lot of artists, and they're always talking about how hard it is to get a place to show their work. A lot of the nicer coffee shops in the city host art shows, and I thought, Horton's could do that."

Sam was smart. The artwork would bring in new customers, and, if any of it sold, Sam would get a share of the price. It seemed crass to mention money, though, and I was sure Sam had motives more lofty than lust for filthy lucre.

"You're like one of those eighteenth-century salon patrons," I told him, "providing a space for art and ideas to flourish."

"Yeah, I've always wanted to do that. That's what teaching was like, for a while."

Cold, fresh whole milk: there's nothing like it. I like it even better than chocolate milk. It is the perfect complement to a Hop on Poppy-seed Muffin, which was what I was having that morning. I licked off my milk mustache and asked, "Why did you quit teaching?"

Sam shrugged. "Lots of reasons. Little things just added up until I knew I had to make a change. I remember one day I found Trina Fenton, the smallest kid in the class, sitting on the floor underneath her desk, sobbing her little heart out. You know what was wrong? Ron Hastings wouldn't be her boyfriend. It was too cruel. Seven years old and she'd already cast herself as Eponine in the *Les Misérables* of second grade. Pathetic. And there was nothing I could do to comfort her. At least here I feed people."

Should I put jam on my muffin, or butter? I preferred butter, but the jam was right there on the counter. I looked through the packets. If there was strawberry, I'd use the jam; if not, I'd ask for butter.

Sam startled me by swiping the salt shaker and talking into it. "Earth to Sam, come in, Sam, you're boring Myr, please terminate current transmission."

"No, you're not," I said. I settled for mixed fruit jelly and opened the packet. "I'm just enjoying the cuisine."

Sam placed a little crock of butter on the counter. "Try this, it's better on those than the jelly."

The butter became one with the fluffy muffin. Then the

buttery muffin became one with me.

Sam said, "Anyway, I'd really like you to bring over a drawing. You're bound to make a sale, not to mention the exposure you'd get."

"Oh, thanks, Sam, but I don't think I have anything ready to show right now." I popped the last sweet muffin morsel in my mouth.

Sam replied without looking at me. He was putting something together below the counter, and his eyes were on his work. "Nonsense. I've seen your sketchbook. You've got real talent. Those sketches you did of the campus in winter? They're sensational! They would sell in a minute! I know *I* would buy one."

"Thanks. I'll think about it. I gotta get going, though. My class starts in fifteen minutes. But before I go, I'd like to order ..."

Sam made a flourish and placed a foil-wrapped package on the counter. "Here you go, Myr. One Fox in Socks Lox and Cream Cheese Sandwich to go!"

I grinned at Sam and said, "I'm very impressed. How'd you know?"

"I wanted you to have some midmorning comfort food," said Sam.

"Thanks. I could use it. I'm having a bad day."

Sam made a big show of checking his Cat in the Hat wristwatch. "Myr," he said, "it's only a quarter to eight in the morning. Don't you think it's a little early to make that kind of judgment?"

I told Sam about Jada and Goat's unscheduled and unorthodox use of the bathroom.

Sam was sympathetic. "Well, you know what they say," he offered. "Eat a live toad for breakfast and nothing worse will happen the rest of the day."

I picked up my sandwich and waved it around. "I think I prefer this." I drained my milk glass, put my money on the counter, and started to go. "See ya, Sam."

"Bring me a drawing," he demanded as the door shut behind me.

Good ol' Sam. After class I curled up on a sun-warmed concrete bench and surrendered myself to the salty lox and the creamy cheese, an appetizer. My next class, biology, wasn't for three hours, plenty of time to gather sustenance for an afternoon of hard study.

Happily, the campus was surrounded by a ring of delis, bakeries, taco stands, and purveyors of fine chocolates. I made several purchases.

 Boston Fern

Curb cuts are important. Not only for wheelchairs and strollers, but for people in my position. I had eaten so much that my tummy bumped against my knees with each step. I needed to take small ones. Preferably toward home.

I navigated my dirigible body back to the house and through the front door. There I was treated to a view of a two-headed, eight-legged creature, part llama, part Goat, undulating on the couch.

"Oh, sorry, guys," I said. "I didn't see you there. I just ..."

I'm glad Margie made me read the *Earth's Children* series by Jean M. Auel. Otherwise I would not have known what was going on in my living room. The books are about Ayla, a member of a goddess-worshipping society that flourished at the dawn of humanity. Ayla furthers civilization in many important ways. She domesticates the horse, invents the bra, and, in chapter after exquisitely detailed chapter, discovers the joy and wonder of human sexuality.

The activity on the couch put me in mind of the passage in which Ayla's boyfriend "tasted her tangy salt."

Jada kept up with her assignments, but she didn't do much recreational reading. Goat read a lot; he always had a copy of *Climber's World* or *Extreme Sports Digest* in his backpack. He didn't read much fiction, though. So it seemed unlikely that either of them had read any Auel. They must have arrived at the idea independently. You had to admire that kind of creativity. Still, it was a poor choice of venue.

"Hey, folks, come on. That's what we have a bathtub for," I said. No answer.

That was okay. I didn't have time to exchange pleasantries. There was homework to be done. I tossed my stomach over my shoulder so it wouldn't drag on the steps and climbed up to my room.

I had five still-life drawings due by Friday morning. I put a mug and a tennis ball on either side of my Boston fern. Then I found my big drawing pad and art-supply box.

I settled in across the desk from the fern composition with a pristine expanse of sketch paper before me, charcoal, erasers, and other supplies at the ready.

I didn't feel like doing the assignment. I leafed through my old drawings instead. In between some uninspired sketches of tables and chairs from last semester was something I had drawn months ago and completely forgotten.

The drawing was of Keith Capri as a satyr, half man, half goat. Done in charcoal, it was all in shades of gray, but even so, the eyes looked sparkling blue. I had seen the subject of the portrait padding shirtless between the bathroom and Jada's door often enough that I could draw his torso very accurately. The figure on the page had muscular shoulders, tiny dark nipples, and a line of curls descending from his navel. Below that he had furry haunches and legs ending in sharp, cloven hooves.

Like the mythological satyrs, the Goat in my drawing radiated sexual energy. He tossed his hair; he pawed the ground. It was probably the most kinetic picture I had ever drawn.

I looked at the picture of Goat. There was more to his nickname than rock climbing. Goats are notoriously rutty animals. And they'll eat anything.

I sketched in a pair of long, arched horns emerging through Goat's curly hair. I finally understood the meaning of the word "horny."

I flipped back to the untouched page. Time to draw the fern. I held my charcoal above the paper and tried to portray light, green, airy. It was no good. I felt heavy, puce, full. I couldn't draw with my jeans cutting into my middle anyway.

I unsnapped, unzipped, and released a cascade of tummy flesh. It was pale, with red marks where it had fought its restraints. I poked one of the welts, and my finger disappeared to the second knuckle.

It reappeared and made for my mouth. A little ridge of fingernail had grown back over the past day or two. The nail snuggled in between my incisors and severed itself from its fingertip.

It played on my tongue for a minute, then was gone. It slipped past my uvula, then down into my gut, where my digestive juices would break it down into its mineral components. They would ride my bloodstream back to my fingertips and be reborn as fingernails once again. It was very spiritual.

Or toenails. I wasn't as flexible as, say, Jada, but I could bite my toenails. I took off my sneakers and socks and checked my right foot.

The right pinkie toe produced the highest overall yield. Its nail wasn't as broad or as hard as the other nails, but it grew quickly, and thicker than the others. I could harvest it nearly every other day.

My teeth came together around it, and the end of my pinkie nail came away gently, as a tulip sheds its petals.

None of the other nine were ready, so I put my socks back on.

Thumbnails were the best, and I tried to keep mine for special occasions. Looking back at the kind of day I'd had, though, I figured I deserved a thumbnail.

My left one had a good six days' growth on it, a pretty white crescent almost level with the end of my thumb. I bit down on the edge of it and started to peel away the stiff keratin, but I'd bitten too low. The nail didn't come off smoothly; it pulled some skin with it. I blew on my thumbnail. It stung.

Color values are very subjective. My belly welts seemed bright red before, but now they looked rosy pink in contrast to the deep red line surrounding my thumbnail.

I sucked my thumb until it stopped bleeding.

Beloved of the Goddess

"You are so lucky to be named Myrtle," Margie opined a few weeks after my first coven ceremony. We were having lunch in the auditorium. We usually avoided the cafeteria and took our brown bags there. I never thought this way about my name, and I couldn't imagine why Margie did. She told me.

"Myrtle is the sacred flower of the Goddess Aphrodite, and you're Myrtle: beloved of the Goddess of Beauty and Love."

"Margie," I said, "I see things a little differently. Let me give you an example. I just came from fourth-period gym. Miss Lubetsky is making us do folk dancing. Of course, the first thing we have to do is pair up, and I'm standing there without a partner."

"I know," said Margie. "It happens to me, too, every time we get to the folk dance unit. Somehow there are always more girls than guys. Did you end up dancing with another girl? That's what I usually do."

"No," I said, "actually, there were four extra guys. None of them would dance with me. I would have been happy to sit out the dance and be in charge of the tape player, but Miss Lubetsky made a really big deal out of it. You know how when she gets excited, her voice gets all sing-songy? Well, she goes, 'Myrtle doesn't have a partner. Now who will be Myrtle's partner?' Like she was coaxing reluctant puppies or something.

"None of those boys is my romantic ideal, but Brian LaSalle is probably the best of the bunch. We're in the same econ class, and he seems to have half a brain. Miss Lubetsky goes up to him and sings, 'Brian, why don't you dance with Myrtle.'

"Brian looks down and shakes his head. I didn't think Miss Lubetsky would let him get away with that, but she went right over to Craig, you know, the one who thinks he's Leonardo DiCaprio?"

Margie nodded and licked her orange fingers. She had almost finished her bag of cheese curls. I took advantage of the pause to unwrap one of my peanut butter and banana sandwiches. They're perfect for school lunches. They have the same flavor and consistency as pb and j, but without the attendant problem of jelly bleeding through the bread after a morning in a hot locker. On special occasions I make them with a crumbled Hershey bar sprinkled over the bananas.

"Yeah," said Margie. "Craig thinks he embodies the spirit of the Horned One, Consort of the Goddess."

"Well, he is conceited, anyway," I continued. "So when Miss Lubetsky asked him to dance with me, he just shook his hair and said, 'I'm not dancing with her.' Naturally this cracked everybody up. I didn't want to see this go any further, so I said to Miss Lubetsky, 'Don't worry about it; I'll dance by myself.'

"Miss Lubetsky repeated what I'd said at triple the volume. 'Dance by yourself? I'm afraid that's unacceptable! This dance requires two people.'

"To which witty Craig replied, 'She *is* two people—weight-wise, that is!' and brought the house down. Tammy Colter laughed so hard she cried and had to run to the locker room and fix her makeup. The guys stood in line to give Craig high-fives.

"I ask you, Margie, does it sound to you like I am beloved of the Goddess Aphrodite?"

Margie made a sound that could have been the quashing of an incipient laugh or the dislodging of a cheese curl. (I'm sure it was a cheese curl. There was nothing funny about the folk dance unit.) I set to work on my sandwiches. They're best when accompanied by a carbonated beverage. I had a bottle of Sprite on hand.

"You are beloved of the Goddess," said Margie. "You *are* the Goddess. You are a formidable woman. Those boys didn't want to dance with you because they feared your power. Your size, your womanliness, is something they both yearn for and fear: yearn for because it is beautiful, fear because it is so different from themselves. They cover up their fear with jokes and taunts.

"Don't let the words of ignorant boys make you feel estranged from the Goddess. Aphrodite is not only the goddess of romantic love; she is Venus, identified with creativity, growth, power, and all the mysteries of the Goddess."

When Margie said "Goddess," her eyes popped out a little, a peculiar but effective form of nonverbal punctuation. I imagined a whole temple full of priestesses in ancient times all popping their eyes every time they said "Goddess." That image and the effervescent soft drink lifted my spirits a little, and I grinned at Margie.

"I can tell," she told me, "you recognize the Goddess within you. Don't lose sight of her."

A Bold Statement

That was the difference between Margie and Jada. Margie thought there was a goddess in every woman. Jada thought that inside every fat woman there was a thin woman crying to get out.

Maybe that was what my nail biting was about: trying to free the thin woman. It was as good an explanation as any, and I'd come up with quite a few: internalized aggression, oral fixation, calcium deficiency. I didn't know why I did it. But it felt good, and it wasn't like it was going to make me go blind.

I had tried to quit a number of times. My last six or seven New Year's resolutions had been to let my nails grow. They never made it past Groundhog Day. I even tried painting them with that bitter-tasting stuff, to condition myself against nail biting. It didn't work. It doesn't really taste all that bad, once you get used to it.

But so what if I bit my nails? I wasn't hurting anybody. I had a pretty little tube of antibiotic ointment that I spread on the occasional infected hangnail. They always healed quickly and cleanly.

They hurt a lot less than my toilet injury. I studied my shin and its oddly shaped bruise. It looked like I'd decided to get a big blue tattoo of Australia. I poked Perth gently. It was tender. I thought about getting a Tylenol. It could do double duty and ease my cramps, too. Margie would not have approved.

I dismantled my fern composition. I would get the assignment done later; now I had other business to attend to. I got my mat knife and a piece of dark blue mat board. I tenderly separated Goat's page from the rest of the sketch book. I measured, marked, remeasured, and cut.

Sam had barely unlocked the door when I burst into Horton's the next morning, lugging my portfolio.

"Good morning, Myr," said Sam. "You're looking sunny

on this misty, moisty morning."

"How do you do and how do you do and how do you do again, Sam?" I answered. Sam had on charcoal-gray slacks and a slate-gray shirt. His tie was teal with a pattern of pink and purple pansies. If Margie had seen it, she would have taken it as a sign that Sam was menstruating.

I shook my head to jostle Margie out of my thoughts. Since I had received that last postcard, everything reminded me of Margie.

I hauled myself onto a stool and balanced my portfolio on the counter.

"So?" Sam ran a finger around the edge of the wide, flat bag. "Do I get to see what's inside?"

I unzipped the portfolio and removed the drawing. Sam was fastidious about keeping Horton's surfaces clean and dry, so I placed the picture squarely before him on the counter. There was Goat, displayed to advantage against a dark blue border.

"You're the first person to see it," I told him.

Sam peered at the drawing. His mustache expanded and spread across his face from dimple to dimple. "Wow, Myr. That is some picture."

He stared at it some more and finally asked, "Is it

for the show?"

I was surprised to notice that my arms were covered with goose bumps. "Yes," I said, "it is."

Sam turned away briefly to get us each a big glass of orange juice. He placed mine on the counter, safely away from the drawing. He carried his around the counter and sat down on the stool beside mine.

"That picture makes a bold statement," he said.

"Oh, you artsy-fartsy types," I joked, "always trying to read bold statements into everything. How cliché. It's just a picture of a guy with goat legs."

"Myr, that is a picture of your roommate's boyfriend." Sam kept careful track of his customers. He knew Jada and Goat, and he knew Jada and I were roommates.

I licked my lips. "This juice is delicious. It tastes just like fresh squeezed," I said.

"It is fresh squeezed," said Sam. "Don't change the subject. We need to talk about this." His mustache sat still and smooth in the center of an earnest expression. "Have you thought about what Goat will say when he sees this picture? What Jada will say?"

I looked again at my drawing. It was more than a realistic rendering of Goat's well-defined upper body. It showed him in motion, muscles rippling, sweat flowing. Looking at it, you could almost hear his heart pounding, feel his breath panting.

I placed my glass on the counter and grimaced. "This orange juice tastes funny," I said. "Maybe you should check the expiration date."

"Myr," said Sam, "I love the picture. I just want you to be sure you're ready to display it."

"Are you afraid it would offend the delicate sensibilities of your customers? Would you prefer that I submit a sketch of a snow-covered administration building?"

"Believe me, it's not my customers' sensibilities I'm worried about. There will be enough other stuff in the show to offend them. One guy is displaying pages of the Bible papier-mâchéd into the shape of a giant hypodermic syringe." Sam chuckled.

"Does the Chamber of Commerce know about your Marxist leanings?" I asked him.

"I think they have their suspicions." He winked at me and continued, "I'm not trying to censor you. You know me; I'm a big fan of the first amendment. I'm happy to include 'Opiate of the Masses,' and I'll be ecstatic to have ... er, what do you call your drawing?"

It worked better written down. I patted my pockets till I found a pen, my pink highlighter. Then I pulled a napkin from the dispenser and wrote down the title. I slid it along the counter to Sam.

He picked it up, read it, and managed to turn his head in time to prevent himself from spraying orange juice on my drawing when he laughed.

The napkin said, "Satyrsfaction."

Imagine the Carnage

"Hi, Myr, what's in the bag?"

Jada gripped her ankles and spoke to me from between her calves. This was the sort of thing she did to keep limber. I dropped my backpack and empty portfolio by the door and flopped into the decrepit green easy chair we had sublet along with everything else that summer.

Wrong decision. Now that I was deep in the chair, it would require considerable effort to stand up again, and my backpack, with my Reese's cups in it, was behind the chair, out of reach.

"Nothing's in the bag," I told her.

Jada let go of her ankles, and they slid apart until her legs were flat against the floor. She stretched her arms out and pressed her palms to the floor in front of her. She spoke into the dusty carpet. "Why'd you carry an empty bag around all day?"

"It wasn't empty when I left this morning. I brought a picture to Horton's for Sam's show."

Jada sat up and turned around to face me. I thought of a llama startled at her grazing.

"You're going to be in a show?" she asked.

"Well, my one picture is, yeah," I said.

"Well, that's terrific news! I always said that if you just put your mind to it you could really accomplish something."

Jada thought she was paying me a compliment. I was supposed to feel flattered.

"When is the opening?" she asked. "This weekend? Let me put up your hair and do your makeup. We are going to make you look beautiful! Let's go upstairs and put together your outfit."

Uh-oh. I knew the look Jada was giving me. It was the look of a llama who wants to give her roommate a makeover. Jada loved giving makeovers. I hated getting them. A makeover was Jada's way of demonstrating to me how offensive I looked without the cosmetics Jada alone had the expertise to apply. Jada had a fairy-godmother complex, and in her version of the story, Cinderella got a sermon about the importance of good nutrition and the impossibility of her ever finding Prince Charming if she insisted on neglecting her skin-care routine.

I got the sermon regularly, but I'd only gotten a full makeover once. When we had been roommies for just a few weeks, Jada thought that with my mature figure and multiple chins, I could buy beer without showing ID. She put primer, a top coat, and detailing on my face until no one would have dared to ask me for ID. They might have asked for my reminiscences of the Reagan era, but they wouldn't have asked for ID.

I never got to test the disguise. About thirty seconds after Jada applied the last layer of shellac to my upswept 'do, some floormates and some guys they'd met in the quad whirled in and swept Jada off to a party where there was beer, free beer for the ladies. I wasn't invited, presumably because they thought I was Jada's elderly maiden aunt who dropped by for a brief visit.

That makeover taught me a lot. Not only did I learn that I should use a very pale foundation and blend it in using a tight spiral motion, I learned that Jada would harass me into makeovers only as long as no one else was around to provide her companionship. That was why I was suspicious of her latest offer to make me look beautiful.

"Aren't you expecting Goat to come over pretty soon?" I asked her.

Still seated, Jada struck a pose with her right foot in her left hand and her left hand over her head. This was her version of a sulk.

"Oh, he went rappelling with Seth. They're camping overnight. He'll be back tomorrow."

Jada shrugged, broke her sulk, and sprang to her feet. "Actually, it's perfect timing. You just got into a show! We can have a ladies-only celebration. I'll make some popcorn. Air-popped, it's only thirty-two calories a cup."

The next thing I knew, I was seated on the scabrous gray carpet in Jada's room while she loomed above me, swabbing Royal Twilight onto my eyelids.

"You're a winter, so you need to wear deeper colors," she told me.

"I am not a winter. My birthday is August thirty-first."

Jada made an impatient gesture with a toadstool-shaped brush. "Please! It doesn't have anything to do with when you were born. It's your coloring. Brown hair, brown eyes, fair skin, that's winter."

"So, if I got chapped skin and bleached my hair, I'd be a springtime?"

"No! You can't change your season. Underlying skin tones are constant, and besides, it's not 'springtime,' it's 'spring.'"

I knew that. Jada had "done my colors" before, and I knew this was a subject about which she felt deeply. My feigned ignorance of seasonal coloring made Jada cross, but I hoped it would keep her from broaching her next-favorite topic: my weight.

It didn't.

"This color really brings out your eyes," she said. "You do have nice eyes, but they're not noticeable because your face is so full. You're lucky, Myr; you have classic features. If you'd just slim down, you could be a real beauty. Uncross your eyes! You're gonna make me mess up your mascara."

"Sorry."

"Seriously, though, you act like you don't even want guys to notice you. Why don't you exercise a little, let your nails grow, put on some lipstick when you go out, maybe get your ears pierced?"

"Oh, I can't stand the sight of blood."

"Don't worry! When you get your ears pierced there isn't any blood, and it only hurts for, like, one second."

"No," I said, "I mean I can't stand the sight of blood shed when men fight over me. It's bad enough now, Jada. Imagine the carnage if I were to lose weight and start wearing makeup and jewelry."

Jada sat back on her heels, tilted her head, and looked at me. Her ears were small and on the sides of her head, but it would have fit in better with her overall look if they had been on top of her head and able to move independently.

She said, "I'm not trying to be mean, Myr. It's just, when I see someone with the potential to look good not do anything with it, it makes me think something is wrong. Look at what a little makeup can do for you."

Some people have big-screen TVs; Jada had a big-screen mirror. It was the size of a small billboard. I had my back to it during the makeover, but, at Jada's bidding, I turned around to meet the new me.

She'd turned me into a kabuki dancer. Well, no, I didn't look like a kabuki dancer, but I didn't look like myself, either. My skin was of a uniform gardenia color, except for two regions of pale pink where my cheekbones must surely have been, and my lips, which were crimson. Jada had been subtle and cunning with Royal Twilight, and my eyes appeared large, dark, and, I dare say, beckoning.

I was an image of luminous beauty. As was only fitting, Margie would have pointed out, since it was my moon time.

"Wow, Jada, uh, thanks." It occurred to me that it might have been more polite of me to look at Jada when I was speaking to her, but I couldn't take my eyes off the vision in the mirror.

Jada jumped up and touched her toes in midair. "Hooray!" she cheered. "I knew you'd like it! Let me do your makeup for the opening, please? Pretty please?"

Jada did a walkover and, with complete control, stopped just short of her big mirror, then dropped down before me in the lotus position.

"C'mon, Myr, you have to. It's not just your art you'll be showing on Saturday. You'll be on display, too. Don't you want to look good?"

Quiche Cups

I decided to have another quiche cup. Sam made these little quiches in mini-muffin tins. Each quiche was about the size of a quarter. They were delicious. I'd had about $2.50 in the first hour of the opening.

Horton's had been transformed. No longer a mere sandwich shop, it was now a stylish art gallery. Where once there hung Thidwick and Bartholomew Cubbins posters, now there were two dozen or more paintings, prints, drawings, and collages. A few sculptures stood on columns that looked suspiciously like tall stools draped with tablecloths.

A large dozing cat painted in blue and green acrylics

shared wall space with a series of watercolor studies of indigenous mushrooms. A carved wooden mask scowled and seemed to be looking sideways at the lithographed landscape beside it. "Satyrsfaction" fit right in, even if I didn't.

I leaned against the wall behind the buffet and watched Sam bring a quiche-laden tray through the crowd. He wore tapered trousers and a coat with tails. Except for the pearly satin stripes on the legs, the whole tux was seashell-pink. A gold watch chain glittered at his waist.

Sam placed the tray on the cloth next to me and puffed air into his mustache. "Whew!" he said. "'Starving artist' isn't just an expression. These folks are eating like Sneetches at a marshmallow toast!" He beamed.

"They sure are enjoying your hospitality," I said. "Why don't you let me help out in the kitchen. I'll make sure the buffet is well stocked."

"Oh, no, I told you before—people love to meet the artists at these things. C'mon, I'll introduce you to ..."

"Sam!" a throaty voice cut in. "You have got to tell me about this monstrous needle!" A woman about Sam's age grabbed him by the arm. She was a summer, so her fuchsia halter top looked great. She led Sam in the direction of "Opiate of the Masses."

I picked up a quiche cup and brought it with me into the bathroom.

Horton's ladies' lounge could accommodate only one lady at a time. I bolted the door behind me. It was my fifth visit that evening. The other four had been primarily for the purpose of killing time. I didn't know anyone at the opening but Sam, and he was too conscientious a host to spend all his time with me. While he was circulating or replenishing refreshments, I divided my time between the buffet and the bathroom. I examined the construction of the stall, played with the soap dispenser, and read the directions on the hot air dryer.

I looked in the mirror and checked my makeup. Not bad. Royal Twilight neither clotted nor caked. I had applied just the right amount. Jada hadn't been home when I was getting ready. She must have forgotten her commitment to the makeover when Goat came back to town.

After searching the sublet for Jada and failing to find her, I realized I was on my own in dressing for my debut. Oh well, at least there would be no chance of Sam's ominous hint coming true at the opening if Jada wasn't even there.

I had changed into clean bluejeans and a black cotton smock with full sleeves and ruffles at the cuffs and neck. It was the fanciest thing I had that still fit. I was still growing. True, I'd been 5'4" for about a year, but I weighed about twelve pounds more now than I had at the start of the summer. The smock was just the thing for an artist who was a growing girl. I went to Jada's room and flapped my sleeves in front of her big mirror.

Behind me, and reflected large as life before me, were Jada's myriad tubes, jars, and boxes of cosmetics. I don't know what came over me. I felt drawn as if by some sinister magnetism to Jada's vanity table. I plundered her store of lotions, creams, and powders, applied them to my face, and set out for the opening.

Ninety minutes later, in Horton's bathroom, I looked upon my makeup job and called it good.

Blam-blam-blam! Someone wanted to knock down the door to the restroom.

It must be her moon time, too, I thought. I opened the door and faced the assailant.

It was Jada.

"Oh, hi, Myr! You look great. We got held up so I couldn't meet you at home first, but we came here right after the movie. Seth and Julie are here, too. Go say hi; I'll be right out."

She stepped past me and closed the door, leaving me

back out in Horton's dining-room-turned-gallery. It happened that "Satyrsfaction" hung on the wall opposite the door to the restrooms. I could see Goat, Seth, and Julie gathered around my drawing.

Interesting acoustics in Horton's; I could hear their conversation from where I stood. But that might have had more to do with their volume than with the way sound traveled in the room.

"So, Goat, you're an inny!" said Julie.

Seth asked, "Myr did that? How'd she get you to pose for it, buddy?"

"Looks like she got every detail," Julie observed.

"Man," said Seth, "she even got your pubic hair! What is she, a nympho?"

"No! She's a psycho!" said Julie.

"I always thought she was a lesbo," said Seth.

"She's a nympho-psycho-lesbo!" Julie shrieked.

It was only ten steps to the door. I took them and was gone before Julie's shriek finished reverberating.

 Blue Salt

"The word 'lesbian' is derived from the island of Lesbos, where the poet Sappho lived almost three thousand years ago. Sappho was so inspirational a poet and thinker that women flocked from all over to study with her. They formed a vital artistic and intellectual woman-centered community. Today the word has an added sexual connotation, but it still means someone who loves women."

Margie paused in her reading and placed her term paper on the coffee table in The Den. It was neatly printed on ten pages of the unbleached 100% recycled paper that Bobbie made us all use. In the style prescribed by our English teacher, the words began halfway down the first page.

ETYMOLOGY & SUBVERSION OF THE PATRIARCHY
By Margie Martin
6th Period English
Mr. Sprenger

Superimposed on these lines of black print was a scarlet let-
ter F, Margie's grade on the paper. Page two bore a ghost F
where the ink from the grade on page one bled through. Mr.
Sprenger had no doubt ruined his felt-tip applying the pres-
sure necessary to make such a mark.

It was Friday evening, not the usual time for our coven
to convene, but Margie had called an emergency session.
Sheila was unable to attend. She was home nursing her
daughter through the latest in a long series of ear infections.
"Perfectly normal for babies her age," according to Sheila's
sources. Thus it fell to me and Bobbie to rally round our
leader in her hour of need. Bobbie had even postponed a
date with her vegetarian beau.

We had spent a portion of the meeting chanting incanta-
tions over salt and trying to dye it blue. Salt and the color
blue, Margie explained, were both symbols of the Goddess,
so blue salt would be very symbolic indeed, just the sort of
charm needed in the current crisis.

Unfortunately, none of us had mastered the technique of mixing salt with food coloring. We quickly ran out of dye and had only a small saucer of blue lumps to show for it. I crumbled them as they dried.

Bobbie shoved aside the salt box and reached for Margie's paper. She flipped through the pages. "No typos, no spelling errors," she said. She turned to the last page. "You put twenty-two books in your bibliography. We only needed to list ten. I can't believe he's not giving you any credit for this."

Margie lit a vanilla candle and shook out the match. "He said that if I turn in a new paper on a 'more appropriate' subject by next Friday, I can still salvage my grade."

Bobbie rolled the paper into a tube and smacked it into her hand. "You only have one week to do a whole new paper? We were given a month to do that assignment," she said.

"It's nothing short of religious persecution," I said and snorted to show my disdain for Mr. Sprenger. Kooky or not, Margie had worked hard on that paper. She deserved better than an F.

"That's why we need to make this charm," said Margie. "Without the protection of the Goddess, Mr. Sprenger might as well burn me at the stake."

"What you need is a couple of faggots," I said.

Margie nodded. Bobbie looked appalled.

"It's in the paper," I said to Bobbie. "Read it."

"You read it," she said, but she was talking to Margie.

Margie took the paper from Bobbie and unrolled it as if it were a sacred scroll. She read aloud, "The word 'faggot,' used today mostly in a pejorative sense, should not be considered an insult but an honor. Faggots fought and died for their beliefs. During the sixteenth century, when witch burning was at its height in Europe and women were being tortured and burned in the hundreds of thousands, some men spoke out against the witch hunts and in defense of their mothers, wives, sisters, and daughters. The patriarchal system that supported the hunts made sure that these men were silenced. They were burned along with the accused women, thrown on the fires like bundles of sticks. Kindling tied in a bundle was commonly known as a faggot. This name was given to these early rebels against a patriarchal culture."

Margie had discussed her paper with me, but this was the first time I'd heard it word for word. I was so absorbed by her dramatic reading that I had been unconsciously dipping my fingers into the blue salt and licking them. My fingers were blue. My tongue and teeth probably were too. This had to be either highly disrespectful of the Goddess or some way of mystically melding with her. I didn't ask Margie which; she was reading her conclusion.

"... and it continues to this day. Any time people threaten the patriarchal hierarchy, by being politically outspoken, physically strong, or spiritually independent, they are called 'lesbians' or 'faggots,' with the implication that these are dirty, sick, shameful things to be."

Margie didn't even look up at us when she finished reading. She just placed the paper face-down on the table and sifted blue salt over it in a spiral design.

I glanced at Bobbie. She smiled uncertainly.

Margie sniffed.

"Margie," I said, "are my teeth blue?"

I bared my teeth, and Margie looked. "Myrtle! Have you been eating the Goddess-crystals?" she asked. She looked alarmed.

"It's very spiritual." I said, "Try it."

Margie licked her finger and pressed it into the saucer. She held up a salty blue fingertip and, with her other hand, pushed the saucer to Bobbie.

Bobbie licked, dipped, and passed me the salt. I followed

their example, and we all three sat, blue fingers pointing toward heaven.

Margie intoned in her ceremonial voice, "As these crystals dissolve within us, we meditate upon the qualities of the Goddess. As we taste the bold flavor of this gift of the Earth, we concentrate on recognizing the Goddess within ourselves."

That said, Margie put her finger in her mouth and withdrew it with a pop. So did Bobbie. So did I. Mystical women's spirituality meets vaudeville.

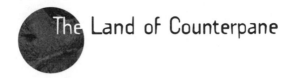The Land of Counterpane

It's when the backs of your eyeballs hurt that you know you've really done it. Mine hurt. I'd done it: consumed ten quiche cups, three chocolate chip cookies, a roast beef sandwich with mustard, one dill pickle, and most of a cheese enchilada. At least binge drinkers get the fun of piecing together memories of the night before and extrapolating the story of what happened from the fragments. Binge eating doesn't affect the memory.

My memory was sharp. Nympho-psycho-lesbo. That Julie had me pegged. I'm a nympho-psycho-lesbo all right. No fooling her.

Hadn't I memorized what Goat looked like without his shirt? Typical nympho behavior.

I propped myself up on my elbows. The backs of my eyes flamed.

I must be psycho. No one but a psycho goes to sleep in a bed full of garbage. I sat up and looked around me. The land of counterpane had been developed by the fast food industry. All up and down among the sheets were bags and wrappers from last night's feast.

A piece of waxy orange paper concealed the end of an enchilada. The cheese was cold and hard. I nibbled at it and investigated the contents of a paper bag by my pillow. Three cookies and a coconut doughnut. It had been the last doughnut in the shop. They threw it in when I bought half a dozen cookies.

My bedspread was at the foot of the bed, wadded up and topped with a big red paper cup. I reached for it and slurped up the last few drops of Coke. There was nothing lonelier, I reflected, than the sound of a straw sucking the dregs of a warm, flat Coca-Cola.

Unless it was the sound of those creeps saying, "Nympho-psycho-lesbo!"

I sighed. If a thin, bejeweled woman with exfoliated skin

and outfits selected to properly complement her seasonal coloring had drawn that same picture, would they have called her a nympho?

No, they'd probably write her up in their alternative newspaper and purchase the drawing for their newsroom. Goat would probably dump his dancer girlfriend and fall madly in love with the artist who had captured his image so perfectly.

Well, that wasn't what I wanted anyway.

What I wanted was a doughnut.

I picked up the bakery bag, but instead of opening it, I crumpled it up and threw it at the door.

The bag hit the door, burst, and rained cookie crumbs and stale doughnut bits all over the carpet. A piñata, aw shucks, and it wasn't even my birthday.

Psycho. Maybe they meant psychic. I sort of thought I might be telekinetic. I mean, I broke that jar of tea without even going near it. And last night, when I came home, the back door blew wide open before I even reached it, which was lucky, since my arms were full of packages. Margie said it. Goddess-energy can influence the physical sphere. Well, that was nice for the Goddess, but right now I didn't even have the energy to influence my physical rear. It wanted to stay in the bed, and I wasn't in the mood to argue with it.

I lay back down and pulled the sheet up over my head. I closed my eyes. I opened my eyes. I pushed the sheet away and gasped. I couldn't breathe under there. The mustard smell was overpowering. I noticed I had gotten mustard on my good black smock. There was a duck-shaped yellow blob drying in the middle of my chest. I swear, every shirt I owned had a stain on the chest, just at the level where my boobs heaved out to catch the food as it fell. Quite a few of my shirts had stains on the tummy, too.

I wondered which stuck out farther, my boobs or my stomach. It had been a close contest for a number of years. I took off my smock, getting a good whiff of mustard as I pulled it over my head, removed my bra, and studied my torso.

The boobs definitely stuck out farther, but it wasn't a fair measure. Half my tummy was confined inside my jeans. I took off my jeans and sat back down, letting my tummy roll out over my knees, like the tides drawn by the moon.

I slapped the surface of Lake Tummy Flesh and watched it ripple. The boobs rippled too. They didn't stick out nearly as far as the stomach, but rested upon it. The shoreline shifted as I brought my left foot up and bent over it.

The big one, the one who went to market, if memory serves, was ready. I bit through the nail and pulled. The state I was in, no wonder I lacked finesse. I tore too fast and too hard and took a morsel of cuticle away with my toenail.

I wrapped the edge of my sheet around my toe and held it, rocking back and forth. It hurt; sure it hurt, but it was a comforting pain.

As long as I was thinking about my poor throbbing piggy, I didn't need to think about Goat or Jada or Seth or Julie or Sam or "Satyrsfaction" or fleeing from Horton's into the night and waking up with a headache in a bed full of garbage.

Takeout from Deli U came in strong bags of opaque green plastic. There was one by my leg. I let go of my foot and grabbed it. I opened it, leaned over, and was sick.

Rascally Bastards

Even my lax standards of housekeeping wouldn't allow me to keep a bag of puke in my room. I put the warm, round sack into a bigger bag with my enchilada end, Coke cup, bakery bag, and other mementos of the previous evening.

I kicked at the laundry scattered around the floor. What to wear? What was the appropriate dress for a jaunt to the outdoor garbage cans? Should I wear the gold taffeta? The black silk? The lavender mohair? No, I'd wear the gray terry cloth. I put on my old bathrobe, cinched it up, and went downstairs with my bundle.

I missed the dorm. I had so much more privacy there. I'd be going back in the fall, to another randomly assigned roommate. Jada had signed up to share Julie's high-rise apartment next year. But until I got back to McLeod Hall, with its formal and informal codes of dorm behavior, I had no reasonable expectation of privacy. I couldn't assume that on an early morning shortcut through the kitchen, dressed only in a bathrobe and underwear, carrying a bag of squishy waste, I wouldn't meet anyone.

"Hey," said Goat. He was seated at the kitchen table, enjoying a nutritious breakfast of baked beans and Mountain Dew.

I've known Mountain Dew to soothe an upset stomach, but the beans, glistening in their red-brown sauce and filling the room with their thick aroma, made me queasy all over again.

Goat pushed his foot against the kitchen chair beside him, so it slid out from the table.

"Hm," he said, which I understood to mean, "Won't you join me?"

It would have been awkward to refuse. I sat down, balancing the trash on my knees.

Goat was dressed today. He had on a turquoise T-shirt and cutoff jeans. No shoes, though. I stared down at his ten tanned toes. He had shiny blond hairs on the biggest ones. His toenails were immaculate, cut straight across with surgical precision.

He saw me looking, and bent his knee so that his right foot was up on the seat of his chair. I looked up.

"Just making sure they're not hooves," I said.

Goat's eyes bathed me in sapphire light, but he didn't speak, just sat regarding the nympho-psycho-lesbo at his table.

"Enjoying your beans?" I asked. They were my beans. Jada didn't keep such offensive stuff in the house. Sure, they were high in fiber, but that sauce they came in—practically nothing but high-fructose corn syrup.

Goat nodded.

"They're good on Italian bread," I said, "with Canadian bacon."

Italian bread, that was good for an upset stomach. I visualized Italian bread, the crunchy crust, the fluffy white middle.

"Yeah," said Goat, "beans rule. They're good to take camping."

"Dried?"

"Huh?"

"When you go camping, do you take dried beans, or canned?"

"Dried. They're lighter."

You're doing fine, I told myself. Draw him out; ask him about his interests.

"Do bears like them?"

"Bears?"

"Dried beans. I mean, I know bears will take campers' food, but they might not even think of beans as food, especially if they're dried and the bears can't smell them. Of course, I've heard that they'll eat dry macaroni, so ..."

I cut myself off. Give the guy a chance to answer, at least.

Goat shrugged. "Don't know," he said. "The bears around here aren't very aggressive. Out west is where they'd steal your food."

This was turning into a regular conversation. It was something, the way we got on so well together.

"How about raccoons?" I asked.

That got Goat excited. He scootched up and leaned over his bean bowl. "Oh, they're little bandits!" he said. "They'll open your pack right up and take whatever's in it."

Goat grinned at the cheek of those rascally bastards. It made his jaw muscles flex.

"Bandits," I said, wittily. We were sharing a moment, Goat and I. Clearly, we were kindred spirits.

He stood up and looked past me. "Hey, Jade," he said.

"G'mornin'," said Jada. She came in and leaned against Goat. He put his hand on her waist and nuzzled her hair.

"Mmmorning," he murmured.

I shouted, "I've heard they wash their food to make it soft because they don't have any saliva glands."

Jada interrupted her snuggle and looked at me. "What are you talking about?" she said.

"Raccoons."

Jada kept staring.

I had never removed last night's makeup. I rubbed my finger under my right eye. It came away smudged with Royal Twilight. I looked down at my shaggy gray robe and checked behind me for a wide, ringed tail.

"You can use cold cream to get rid of that," said Jada, "but it stings if it gets in your eyes, so I like to use baby oil. Just put a little on a cotton ball, but remember always to use a gentle downward motion; otherwise you're just pushing all that makeup and oil right back into your pores."

She took a step toward me, and I had the crazy idea that she was going to spit on a tissue and wipe my face with it.

I stood up and backed away. Then, since, of course, Jada was planning on doing no such thing, I had to make my retreat look casual. I sidled toward the door.

"I was just on my way to take out the trash," I told them.

As if they cared. They were kissing; little squeaky pecks on lips, cheeks, ears, foreheads.

I went outside.

When I came back in, there was no sign of Jada or Goat but the bean residue in the bowl on the table. I climbed back up the stairs.

I paused at the top. A llama had passed this way, followed by a Goat. They had turned right and were now behind Jada's closed door.

I turned left, into the bathroom. Hadn't Jada implicitly given me permission to use her baby oil and cotton balls? I thought so. So she certainly wouldn't mind my using her bubble bath and rosebud-shaped scented soaps.

She had an inflatable pillow with a suction cup on the back to make it stick to the side of the tub. I took it out and blew it up. It came with a loofah mitt, which looked new. No sense in letting it go to waste. I unwrapped it and dropped it into the bathtub.

Jada's shampoo was in the soap dish. It was a special

formula—fifteen dollars a bottle—made for curly hair. Mine is straight, but I was feeling reckless. I lathered up.

The shampoo bubbles were different from the bubble-bath bubbles, white and foamier. The bubble-bath bubbles were big and colorful. I made a sculpture: tiny shampoo bubbles piled on top of larger bubble-bath bubbles, piled on top of the big balloons of my breasts floating half in, half out of the water.

I liked the repeated round shapes. That would be something fun to draw. I could call it "Still Life with Boobs."

I filled the loofah mitt with water and poured it over my masterpiece, rinsing it away.

I loofahed my arms and shoulders. It felt great. I hummed to myself as I scrubbed my neck and chest. In the water, my skin looked as white as the bathroom tile; breaking the surface, it flushed and gleamed in the steam.

I took off the mitt and massaged the rosebud soap into thick pink suds. I spread the suds across my tummy and up my sides, like frosting on the world's biggest strawberry cake.

When I leaned back on the bath pillow, most of the soap was submerged. It detached and floated on the surface for a while before it dissolved.

I looked past my boobs, over my stomach, and out to my thighs in the distance beyond. There wasn't a sharp angle or a jutting bone for miles.

Everything was soft, curved, round.

"Round," I said. You had to make your lips into a circle to say it.

"Rowwwnd," I enunciated.

I said it under water. "Rowwwnd-blub."

The special shampoo instructions said, "Lather, rinse, repeat." I repeated.

I didn't get out until the water was cold and the bubbles had all gone flat.

Nasal Discharge

Horton's was closed on Sundays, but Sam usually came in around 2:00 to do paperwork and spiff the place up.

I went around to the back door and peeked in the window. Sam was polishing the stainless steel milk cooler and boogying to some synthesized music. I let myself in.

"Bananarama!" Sam said when he saw me. "These ladies were the Supremes of the 1980s."

I hoisted myself onto a stool and leaned my head on my arms at the counter.

Sam turned the music down. "Guess how many people came to the opening last night, Myr. Two hundred! Maybe more. That's an estimate based on the guest book, but of course not everybody signs it, so I rounded up, but, still, I'm trying to be conservative."

"Yeah, Sam, that's exactly how I'd describe you: conservative."

"Conservative? Moi? Au contraire. I exist on the radical fringe of the art world. I fraternize with—" Sam looked around as though to make sure we were truly alone, then whispered, "—Marxists!"

He smiled and looked past me. I followed his gaze to the glossy yellow tag affixed to the pedestal beneath "Opiate of the Masses." SOLD, it said.

"Sam!" I said in a whiskey-and-cigarettes voice, "you have got to tell me about this monstrous needle." I sounded just like the lady of the fuchsia halter top. "Who was she, anyway?"

"Lauren Toth. She's an old friend. You might have seen her around campus. She's chair of the Women's Studies Department."

"Did she buy the sculpture?"

"No, someone from the Economics Department beat her to it. By the way, she loved your drawing."

"Satyrsfaction" was just where I'd left it. I averted my eyes. I didn't want to see it. I didn't want to talk about it.

Sam explained, "I wanted to introduce you to Lauren, but I didn't see you around. Did you leave early?"

I grabbed a napkin from the dispenser. My eyes were watering. My nose was running.

"Uh-oh. What'd I miss?" asked Sam.

"Jada and Goat's friends," I said. "Seth and Julie. They saw the drawing I made, and they said ... they said ..."

Sam handed me a wad of napkins. I blew my nose.

"They said I was a nympho-psycho-lesbo."

Good ol' Sam. He kept a straight face. "That's ridiculous," he told me. "You're not a lesbo."

I laughed and got nasal discharge on my face. Sam gallantly pretended not to notice. I used up another handful of napkins.

"You know what I'd like?" Sam asked brightly. "A pot of my special Mulberry Street Blend tea. Care to join me?"

"Thanks, Sam."

Mulberry Street was an herbal blend of chamomile, peppermint, and a secret ingredient—mulberries, I guess. Sam handed me a mug, and I inhaled the spicy steam.

Sam said, "What those guys said isn't so bad. They could have called you a lot worse than 'lesbo.'"

"Like, f'rinstance, 'nympho-psycho?'" I asked.

Sam smiled. "Well, yeah, that's worse. But people like Seth and Julie think 'lesbo' is the worst insult in the world."

I thought so too, but I didn't want Sam to think I was a heterosexist pig.

Sam raised his mug and said, "Congratulations, Myr. You're part of a grand tradition of individuals who threaten the status quo and are thus branded dykes and faggots!"

"Sam, the language."

Sam colored up till he matched his salmon polo shirt. He picked up the teapot and freshened my mug of Mulberry Street Blend. "Sorry."

"That's okay. You sound like this girl I knew in high school."

"Really? Who?"

"Her name was Margie Martin. People thought we were a couple."

Class Couple

"A couple o' what?" said Sam. He tapped the ash off an imaginary cigar and waggled his eyebrows.

"A couple of dykes!" I answered, louder than I had to. I hopped off the stool and paced around. "She didn't care if people thought we were lesbians. She used to say that all women were lesbians because the life force was female and so, if you loved life, you loved women."

"Can't argue with that kind of logic," said Sam.

"We didn't have boyfriends. We didn't wear makeup. Margie didn't even shave her legs."

I didn't either, but since I always wore jeans, no one knew. Margie favored long swirly skirts that wafted around and exposed her fuzzy shins.

"We sat together all the time," I explained. "We wrote each other notes. At our school that was like wearing pink triangles and waving rainbow flags."

"You're not serious."

It was true. I remembered one of the more spirited discussions in our senior history class which proved it.

"Antony and Cleopatra," said a classmate, and Mrs. Vinton wrote it on the board.

"Good answer. Any others?" she said.

"Romeo and Juliet," someone offered.

"Well, they're fictional, but okay. Who else?"

"Grace Kelly and Prince Rainier."

"Excellent example. Come on, you can think of some more. Who have been the most romantic couples in history?"

Tug Dougherty answered, "Margie and Myrtle." His minions whooped and guffawed.

Mrs. Vinton frowned. "Let's confine our discussion to historical figures."

I'd been doodling a design of leaves and flowers around the border of my paper. I couldn't think of a reason to participate in this discussion, so I kept drawing.

I didn't look at Margie, but I heard her chair slide back

when she stood up.

"Gertrude Stein and Alice B. Toklas. Eleanor Roosevelt and Lorena Hickok."

"Um, Margie ..." said the teacher.

"These are the most romantic couples I know, Mrs. Vinton. I'm only trying to answer the question."

"Margie, sit down." Mrs. Vinton's voice had an edge of impatience now.

"Why? You asked us to come up with a list of romantic couples. I'm listing them. Rita Mae Brown and Martina Navratilova. Margaret Wise Brown and Blanche Oelrichs."

"Margie, shut up!" I'd thought I was whispering, but my voice wasn't too low for Tug's keen ears.

"Woooo, lovers' quarrel," he hooted.

"That's enough! All of you!" Mrs. Vinton tried, and failed, to regain control of the class.

"It's scary, isn't it, Tug?" asked Margie. Her voice had that ceremonial formality. Within The Den it was a little silly, but here in history class, it was kind of spooky. "Pretty frightening to think that women might enjoy each other more than they would you. You'd rather joke about it than consider the awesome power of women loving women."

Though Tug was not a member of the debate team, he

nevertheless was ready with a pointed reply. "Friggin' dykes," he said.

My doodled border looked splendid. The margin was burgeoning with flowers and leaves, fruits and tendrils.

Mrs. Vinton said, "Tug, you're pushing it. Margie, please. Sit down." She did a little deep breathing, then addressed the class. "You have twenty minutes to start on your homework. The rest of the period is study hall. I want you to read chapter twelve. In silence."

"I am serious," I told Sam.

I drank some more tea, and the herbal blend suddenly seemed insipid. I needed caffeine. I was tired, so tired I wanted to go to bed and sleep till morning. Maybe longer.

"And who the hell was Margaret Wise Brown?"

"Pardon?" said Sam.

"According to my old school chum, she was some famous lesbian. But I've never heard of her."

"Yeah, you have," said Sam. His eyes were actually gleaming. "She probably put you to bed every night when you were little."

I was really not in the mood for Sam's zany madcap humor. "Never mind. I'm sorry I asked," I said.

"No, really," Sam said, his face alight with reverence. "She wrote children's books. They're classics. You must have seen them. *The Runaway Bunny*? *Goodnight Moon*?"

Again with the moon. No wonder Margie liked her.

Sam quoted from memory. "Goodnight bears."

I yawned. I couldn't help it.

"Goodnight chairs."

I laid my head down on the counter. The memory of that history class was still playing behind my eyelids. I watched it.

Refuge,  Safety, Haven

I disappeared from class as soon as the bell rang. Margie caught up to me in the hallway and said, "I'm disappointed. I don't think you demonstrated sisterhood with me in there."

I kept walking. People are surprised by how quickly I can walk. I'm not long-legged, I'm not athletic, but I can really move when I've got someplace to go. Or someone to get away from. But Margie kept pace. She is long-legged.

"I mean, I didn't expect you to argue with Tug, but did you have to tell me to shut up?" she said.

I bolted, head down, a boulder rolling down the halls of Seneca High School.

Margie said, "That's the way of the patriarchy: divide and conquer. Women submit to hierarchical structures only once they cease to depend on and trust one another. Standing up to oppression requires that we support each other." She paused, then added, "That means not telling me to shut up in front of a room full of people."

Up ahead—refuge, safety, haven: the school library. "I'm going in here," I said. "I've got study hall."

"I'll go with you."

I stopped in front of the library doors. "No. You can't come with me. You're always with me. People think we're always together. It's embarrassing."

"How can it be embarrassing? We're supposed to do things together. We're friends."

What was I going to tell her? That I wanted to see less of her because Tug, whose opinion I so valued, thought we might be lesbians? I was tired of the Goddess, weary of lunar metaphors, sick to death of the sacred symbolism of the menstrual cycle.

"It's not just that," I said. "It's all the witchy stuff. It's bizarre. People think we're freaks."

"No, they don't. Look at Bobbie," said Margie. Bobbie, by this time, had been a member of the homecoming court and had convinced the hospitality committee to have meatless Not Dogs available at the concession stand for the football games.

"Bobbie's not like us," I said. "She has other friends and activities. You may have noticed she's missed a few coven meetings lately?" She'd missed, maybe, the last ten.

"Bobbie is exploring her selfhood," said the magnanimous Margie.

"Yes, and I'm sure the Goddess is tremendously honored by that, but, you know, Bobbie somehow manages to honor the Goddess without standing up and listing famous lesbian couples of history and embarrassing her friends," I said.

"I embarrassed you?" asked Margie. "Tug's the one who called us a couple. I was disarming him. If we celebrate homosexuality instead of condemning it, his barb has no sting."

It stung. It was still stinging! Why couldn't she see that?

I tried to keep my voice quiet. "People think we're lesbians, Margie. Doesn't that bother you?"

"No, it doesn't. I want to transcend the narrow gender and sexual roles defined by the patriarchy. I refuse to be labeled gay or straight."

"Well, I'd very much like to be labeled straight, but it

seems the only label ever applied to me is 'Margie's fat friend.'"

"In ancient times," said Margie, "there wasn't such emphasis on whether people were gay or straight. Sexual union was an homage to the Goddess. That's what I strive for. I've kept myself pure in her honor."

I forgot to keep my voice quiet. "That's great!" I shouted. "Maybe you can be the guest speaker at the next Seneca High Spiritual Youth for Abstinence meeting. I bet they've never had a pagan presenter before."

"Good idea," said Margie, but she hadn't been listening. She was off again. "I'm thinking we could have a ceremony about that, about how the Goddess is the ultimate source of love, so loving women—not just as lovers, but as sisters and friends, too, you know—honors the Goddess and honors ourselves. We could bring in photographs or drawings of women we admire, and cast a spell ..."

Margie went on blithely, as if she hadn't just humiliated me, as if she were back in The Den, as if I gave a bloody menstrual rag about anything she had to say right now.

I cut her off. "Margie, you can't cast a spell. You're not a witch. You're not a priestess. You're a weird teenager who burns a lot of candles. If there ever was a Goddess religion, it's been dead for thousands of years. You can't bring it back by making charms in your basement."

Margie had been styling herself a latter-day witch and Goddess worshipper for so long that I thought she had no other persona. Her formal speech, her stately gait, her incessant references to ancient ways were simply part of who she was. Watching all those affectations fall away was like watching Margie dissolve.

She hung her head and slouched against the wall. Her voice sounded reedy when she said, "I thought you liked the coven. You don't have to come anymore if you don't want to."

I didn't. I never returned to The Den. I stopped taking my lunch to the auditorium. I graduated without benefit of a coven benediction, and went to college 100 miles away from Seneca High School and 500 miles away from the ivy-encrusted institution where Margie matriculated.

But early freshman year (frosh year, as Margie called it, in her effort to avoid sexist language), Margie sent me a postcard. After that there were e-mails, a handmade Halloween card, and more postcards, two or three a semester.

"Hello," they said. Or they'd give news about the weather or what classes she was taking. They said nothing spiritual or mystical or menstrual.

"Here you go," said Sam, placing another napkin dispenser beside the one I'd emptied. I helped myself to some more napkins. My eyes and nose wouldn't stop leaking.

"I'm okay," I told him, "just tired."

I'd only had my head down for a minute. Maybe I'd just go home and take a nice little sixteen-hour nap.

I thanked Sam for the tea and trudged out, my pockets bulging with snot-soggy napkins.

Two by Two

It's not like the bookshop was out of my way. I had to go within two blocks of it to get back to the sublet anyhow.

The front of the store was crowded with alumni busily acquiring keychains, sweatshirts, and coasters in school colors, but the back of the store, where the books were, was deserted. The kids' books were in a display case shaped like Noah's ark, with stuffed animals on the shelves, two by two.

There were bears, cats, ducks, elephants. Either I was reading too much into this or someone had arranged the toys in alphabetical order. Luckily, they'd done the same with the books, so it wasn't hard to find Brown, Margaret Wise.

I ran my fingers over the spine of *Goodnight Moon* and took down a copy of *The Runaway Bunny*. The first page showed a black and white drawing of a big rabbit chasing a little one. He was running away, and she vowed to run after him.

That little bunny did everything he could to get away from his mother, but she always stayed with him. If he turned himself into a fish, she turned herself into a fisherman. If he turned himself into a sailboat, she turned herself into the wind.

What was it with her? She just wouldn't let up. Couldn't she tell that the little bunny didn't want anything to do with her anymore?

What was I missing here? When I had asked Sam about Margaret Wise Brown, he nearly burst into song with his enthusiasm, but I just didn't get it.

I sat down on the floor with *The Runaway Bunny* and flipped the pages back to front.

Oh, I got it. It had to be the little bunny's blue-striped pajamas. I had never seen Sam in his intimate apparel, but as surely as I knew the taste of Butter Battle Batter Griddle Cakes, I knew Sam would covet those pajamas.

Toward the end of the book, the little bunny was

cuddling up in his mother's lap after another thwarted attempt to run away. He was wearing snazzy blue-on-blue striped pajamas. He and his mother were rocking, nose to nose, by the fireplace.

He didn't really want to run away from her. He just wanted to assert his independence a little.

It was nice to know she would always be there for him, even if he turned himself into a fish. Or a bird, or a rock, or a sailboat.

Even if he made fun of her religion. Even if he told her to shut up in front of all the other bunnies. Even if he never answered her e-mail or postcards.

That mother bunny was always there, a steady presence. She loved him. Unconditionally.

"Excuse me."

I snapped the book shut.

"Sorry, ma'am, but we're closing. We're only open till four o'clock on Sundays."

The clerk wasn't any younger than I was, but I wasn't really surprised he called me ma'am. I'd been addressed that way since I was fourteen. It was the hips. Or maybe the chins.

"Ma'am?" said the clerk. I wondered if he was the one

who had alphabetized the animals. He bent slightly and held out a hand.

Oh, come on! One minute I was "ma'am," the next I was a suspected shoplifter? I gave him a sarcastic smile and handed over *The Runaway Bunny*.

He put the book in his other hand and still held one out to me. "We're closing," he said again.

That was sweet—no lever, no pulley system. He thought he could just extend his hand and help me up.

He weighed about as much as my left arm. If I accepted his offer, he would crumple right down to the floor before I budged an inch. The image cheered me, and I grasped his hand.

Up I went. His bony little fingers pressed into the back of my hand and pulled me into a standing postion.

He offered me *The Runaway Bunny*. "The cashier is open for five more minutes, if you want to get that," he said.

I did.

Gusto

I went back to the sublet, up the back steps, across the porch, and into the kitchen.

Jada was there, spooning unsweetened yogurt into the blender.

"Hi, Myr, look. I got blueberries. Take one."

She held the box out to me, and I took a couple. They were good. She shook about half the berries into the blender and put on the lid.

"Hey, Goat," Jada shouted at the ceiling, "want a smoothie?"

Silence.

"He must still be sleeping," she said.

It was almost 4:30 in the afternoon.

"What's that?" asked Jada, gesturing at the bag from the campus bookstore.

I slipped the book out onto the table. "It's a kid's book, a classic."

"*The Runaway Bunny*. Hmm. What's it about?"

It's about me and Margie, I thought. "Rabbits," I said.

Jada looked as if she might ask me why I had a picture book about rabbits, if it were a subject worth pursuing.

Instead she asked, "You want a smoothie?"

"Sure, thanks."

Jada blended and poured, and pretty soon we were seated companionably at the kitchen table with our glasses. I took a sip. It was disgusting, thick and bitter, with strands of berry skin running through it. Jada drank hers with gusto.

"You know, you let things get to you too much," she said.

"Yeah, I've heard that."

"Last night at Horton's, I came out of the bathroom, and I'm like, 'Where's Myr?' and they're like, 'She left,' and I'm like, 'Why?' and they told me." Jada gulped some smoothie. "I'm like, 'I can't believe she left.'"

"Yeah, well, I can't believe how rude your friends are."

"They didn't mean anything by it. You should have

stayed. We had a great time. There was this one professor there wearing a pink halter top and, like, five-inch heels. She told the raunchiest jokes."

"So I'm supposed to stay and pal around with your friends who think I'm a nympho-psycho-lesbo?"

"Well"—Jada interrupted herself to take a drink—"I'm sorry, but you kind of asked for it. I mean, you draw Goat like he's some kind of sex-crazed animal. What are they supposed to think?"

I wondered if smoothie would stick to llama fur. "You know what?" I said. "I don't care what they think. So what if I am a psychotic nymphomaniac lesbian? It's none of their business!"

I didn't care for Jada's superior little smirk when she said, "Then why'd you leave?"

I stood up, crashing my chair into the wall behind me. "Because," I screamed, "I am so sick of it! It's like nothing matters but the size of my ass. Isn't that what they were saying? How ridiculous it is for someone so fat to draw such an erotic picture?" On "fat" and "picture" I stamped my feet, causing the smoothies to tremble in their glasses.

Jada didn't tremble. She looked at me with her wide, mild eyes and spoke with exaggerated clarity, as if addressing a slow learner. "Myr, they were kidding."

They weren't kidding. But I shouldn't have left. I should have placed my intimidating girth between them and "Satyrsfaction" and challenged them to draw something better. That paper of theirs used photos and clip art, but no original illustrations. I was sure neither of them could draw water from a faucet.

"You have to admit," Jada added, "it was pretty funny. I mean, who would have believed you had a thing for Goat? You're really not his type."

I took a sip of smoothie and remembered why I hated it. It tasted like sludge.

"Jada," I said, "are you mad at me for drawing that picture? I understand if you are. Goat is your boyfriend."

Jada let loose the laugh she had been holding in. "Myr! You're not exactly a threat!"

Blue Moon

Jada's mirror saw it all: brown hair, brown eyes, one big brown eyebrow, one dimple, two chins, no visible collarbones, a monolithic middle, and thighs like the standing stones at Avebury.

Canvas sneakers, faded jeans, stained T-shirt, industrial-strength bra, and cotton panties were all in a heap, off to the side. Honest Abe, creased and spindled, nestled in a pocket. Margie's postcard. The postmark was a week old.

I didn't expect Jada and Goat back any time soon. They were out with Seth and Julie.

It had taken a thorough excavation of my closet, but I'd finally found what I needed: a jar of blue finger paint.

Pardon me, woad finger paint.

Margie had once suggested painting ourselves woad (that is to say, blue) in what she swore was an ancient rite of strength-claiming. Other coven business had forestalled the plan, and it was never carried out. We had all gotten jars of woad, though. I wondered if Margie and Bobbie still had theirs. Sheila, I was sure, had long since given hers to Jilly.

I held the jar in the beam of late-afternoon sunshine streaming in the window. When I swirled the container, the paint sloshed up the sides of the glass and dripped down slowly. It was just the color of the ocean waves in *The Runaway Bunny*.

I unscrewed the lid from the paint jar and dipped my finger into the paint. It was thick and smooth and cold, like cerulean pudding.

I put a blue dot on my nose and outlined my eyes with more paint. I put a big blue circle in the middle of my forehead, and a smaller circle on my chin (the first one). I checked my reflection. Jada was right. Makeup really did change my look.

With slippery blue fingers, I covered my legs and thighs with flowers and geometric patterns. My belly and breasts became a vast seascape, with a blue moon on my sternum shining a path to my navel.

My arms and shoulders matched my thighs, festooned with stars, circles, and spirals, as well as flowers of every description.

I looked into the mirror, twisting side to side to better see my whole canvas.

I knelt on the floor in front of the mirror. Jada's carpet took on some circles and stars when I did that, but at the time I didn't notice. I was looking at my reflection.

"Hi," I said, "I recognize you."

I reached out and pressed the glass. My reflection, of course, did the same thing.

"Don't go away. I'll be right back," I told her. I left and was back a minute later with my big sketch pad, an easel board, some brushes, and a jar of water.

I swished a paintbrush through the water, then dipped it into the paint.

Hours later, I shuffled back to my room, carrying my stuff and being careful not to let the wet paper touch my body.

I put my comfy terry cloth robe on over my woad-coated skin. I set my new painting on the desk to dry. I took a piece of mat board from under my bed and placed a new blade in my knife. I measured, marked, remeasured, and cut.

Sam had barely unlocked the door when I burst into Horton's the next morning, lugging my portfolio.

"I'll trade you," I said to him. "Give me back 'Satyrsfaction,' and I'll hang up what's in the bag in its place."

"Who are you? Monty Hall?"

"Who's that?"

"Never mind. Why don't I get to keep 'Satyrsfaction'?"

"I'm giving it to Jada."

Sam looked incredulous.

"I am."

"Why?"

I shrugged. "She's my roommate."

Sam put his hand on his chin and looked at "Satyrsfaction." He tilted his head to the right, then to the left. "You know, you could still sell it," he said finally.

I patted my portfolio. "I have something else for the show," I said, "something better."

"Better than 'Satyrsfaction'?" Sam said. "You must have smuggled in a Picasso, a Cassatt, a Renoir, a Geisel!"

Myrtle of Willendorf

Visitors to the Women's Studies suite in Walker Hall will now be greeted by the art of sophomore Myrtle Parcittadino, whose watercolor painting "Myrtle of Willendorf" was recently purchased for $500.00.

Reaction to the purchase has been mixed. Women's Studies senior Beth Hughes says, "I'm not sure hanging a picture of a big naked woman in the Women's Studies office promotes the kind of image we want the department to have."

"Oh, you old flatterer," I said. "Okay, take a look."

I unzipped my portfolio and revealed my painting. As soon as it was dry, I'd mounted it and brought it over to Horton's.

Sam looked from the painting to me and back to the painting. "Holy Who-ville," he whispered.

"Thanks, Sam," I giggled. I knew he meant it as a compliment.

"So, do we have a deal?" I asked him.

"Hmm? Oh, yeah. Yes. Take it. Here." Sam took "Satyrsfaction" gently but firmly from its wire. I put my new painting in its place.

Dear Margie,

Thanks for your postcard. I know I haven't been the greatest pen pal of all time, but I'm turning over a new leaf. From now on, I promise to write or e-mail you regularly, I swear to Goddess!

Remember our coven? I've been thinking about it a lot lately, as you can probably tell from the enclosed clipping.

Are you going home for Labor Day weekend? Maybe we can get together. I'd like to see you.

Your friend,
Myr

Women's Studies Department chair Lauren Toth supports the department's selection. She says, "Parcittadino's art threatens our preconceived notions of beauty, emphasizing the diversity of that which we call female."

Toth saw the painting at Horton's Omelette Shoppe and Gallery on Campus Street, where it was a late entry into the current show.

"I've known Myr for almost a year now, and I can tell she has heart, wit, and immense talent," says Horton's proprietor, Samuel Horton.

Parcittadino herself has little to say about the controversial piece. "It is sort of a self-portrait," she says. The title, says Parcittadino, is a reference to the Willendorf Venus.

Discovered in Willendorf, Austria, it is one of several mysterious carvings thought to be artifacts of a pagan society that flourished thousands of years ago.

The painting can be seen at Horton's until the end of the summer term, when it will go into the Women's Studies office, 110 Walker Hall.

Photo caption: Myrtle Parcittadino poses next to her self-portrait, "Myrtle of Willendorf."